Going It
Alone

Also by Russell Sullivan

Everything needs a beginning, and this book was the second by this author, the first to be published.

Its predecessor was A Question Of Intelligence and one day perhaps it will make its way into readable form.

In the future, should publishing warrant it, a web-site for PAUONH the authors publishing entity named after a defunct entity The Petrograd Amateur University Of Natural History consigned to history for borrowing a name. One day history may resurrect itself and make this publicly available.

This is the beginning . . .

And the author shall continue "Going It Alone"

Going It Alone

Russell Sullivan

BALBOA.
PRESS
A DIVISION OF HAY HOUSE

Balboa Press books may be ordered through booksellers or by contacting:

Balboa Press
A Division of Hay House
1663 Liberty Drive
Bloomington, IN 47403
www.balboapress.com.au
1-(877) 407-4847

ISBN: 978-1-4525-0942-6 (sc)
ISBN: 978-1-4525-0943-3 (e)

Printed in the United States of America

Balboa Press rev. date: 03/14/2013

Acknowledgements

All persons, places and events in this book are fictional. Any resemblance to those living or deceased is entirely coincidental.

This is for those who do not seem to fit in, or 'belong'. It is not necessarily a bad thing; actually it can have its benefits. So rather than being 'joiners' they live, work and play outside those usual formal groups and establishments.

Going it alone for some may seem a dangerous or lonely choice. For others it is their natural way. Is there a downside? Everything has a downside. Is there an upside? Well there is an element of freedom, a lack of argument and perhaps that little bit of adventure or sense of exploration. Not exactly devil may care, but que sera sera.

So to those who go it alone, and say to hell with it, it is only life and I will give it a try.

Good luck to you.

Contents

NOWHERE

So, where am I?

Nowhere.

That is not so unusual; come to think of it there is a sense of familiarity about it.

It is not bleak, stark nor barren.

Nowhere is simply devoid of many of what people would consider to be usual things.

In a strange way it is quite beautiful, in another way it is quite dark. The mind needs to sort out these and decide which it is, and this is not an easy task.

The question most sensibly could be asked, how does a person find themselves Nowhere?

How to answer that.

An atlas provides a display of all those places on this Earth that are both inhabited and uninhabited. This can be further limited to those places upon this Earth that are unexplored.

The unexplored being ever so gradually reduced over time as the intrepid nature of humanity encroaches and investigates our home planet.

There were halcyon days many a year ago when the deeds of those who sought to understand nature's mysteries, or sought to extend the boundaries of their existence into new territories were the stuff of legend.

These people by their very deeds forging for themselves a place in society and the minds of those who inhabited it.

Bygone days.

This is the now, and such deeds are no longer commonplace, nor do they necessarily command the same level of attention.

How then a person finds themselves Nowhere would seem to be an even more remote possibility.

Only to those who inhabit the norm.

Prior to progressing it is necessary for the sake of clarity to understand 'the norm.'.

Is it a place?

Is it a type of person?

The answer is neither and both. A sort of simultaneous equation that permutates everyday existence.

This Earth depicted within the atlas pages contains such a profundity of existence that, like a congested smoker it imperils itself.

Does this concern the inhabitants of this Earth?

Such a question is best directed toward the smoker, and those who seek to rid society of what they would consider to be a blight.

Already a dichotomy is becoming clearer.

So the norm now has at a minimum two separate groupings. These groupings multiplying and cascading like the tree of life into multifarious entities each struggling to find its niche.

A veritable cascade that tumbles across the face of the planet and crashes with the force of a mighty torrent into everyday life.

With such ferocity does this torrent rage it is understandable why nature forges such a strong will from its charges.

Amidst it all though one should also heed the gentle chirruping of those droplets that are gently carried along by life's' current. There is as much beauty within the tree of life to admire and give pleasure as there is peril.

Mighty peaks may humble even the most skilled climbers, yet those same peaks strike awe and almost reverence from those who gaze upon them.

All this seeks to clarify where somewhere is.

That place inhabited and existed in by the norm. And that place that itself represents the norm. Gradually expanding over time as those deeds of humanity in exploring both nature and this Earth have forged a stronger bond between humanity and its home.

This bond has grown as humanity has thrust nature under its foot crushing plague, famine and foe in humanities relentless quest to not only survive, but to flourish.

Has this created a sense of arrogance, possibly? Has humanity bludgeoned nature to the extent that now those misapprehensions of early years are replaced by a sense of supremacy?

The victor and the vanquished.

All from the smallest virus to the dark jungle depths slowly falling victim to humanities progress.

Conquered.

There is resistance of course.

This Earth and its inhabitants neither yielding readily to the challenges of this on-going battle.

The battle of existence.

Now you understand how it is, those who seek to and participate in this battle find themselves somewhere.

How you end up Nowhere will need to wait.

COMPETITIA

Oh come ye forth

on dragons of steel

come ye forth

grist for the mill

Do ye not see?

is it beyond the ken?

look behold

what will begin?

Eyes piercing glare

hopes glimmer dismay

see the day

hear the pain

'Tis competitia

do you not play?

what outcome

no matter

Competitia is all

competitia

'tis your day

PROCLIVITY

There is a tendency, or seems to be a tendency amongst some toward, well almost anything it would seem.

As moths are inexorably drawn toward the light of a candle, so others are drawn toward activities and actions to sate their desires.

What is it you yearn for?

Is it a dark desire, a passion to be fulfilled?

These questions are not necessarily as important as they may seem. While motivation and aspirations make and unmake many a person demotivation is as much a factor.

So for some there is a role in life as opposites; negatives. Negatives that are positives, or so they would consider themselves. And these same people have a tendency, or proclivity toward considering themselves in this manner.

"Doctor" the patient enquires "what ails me so?"

This is a serious question, and dependent upon the type of malady may be an imploring statement or simply form of complaint.

The Doctor will note the tone and decide accordingly, for it is interesting that for some a plea is issued for the most minor complaint, while others may sniff derisively at more dangerous ailments.

A Doctor comes to know their patients, like a teacher comes to know their pupils. So there is an art, and an almost sinister art in deciding what is appropriate, and what may be appropriate may be at odds with the inner concept of the patient.

This is a dangerous course, for dissatisfaction is a most likely result. The patient or pupil may seek an alternate source to nourish this desire. A more caring, nurturing source not so easily wheedled or perhaps cajoled.

For it is true, in those more dire cases where desire trammels the heart of the patient, or pupil, request may become demand.

And like a faithful dog they will perch themselves, unmoving and unmovable on the steps of those who seek to provide remedy for what ails them.

In so doing their ailment becomes apparent.

The treatment, like the faithful dog may seem callous. Cast out and unsatisfied it is possibly they will retaliate, seek recompense for the rebuke.

Others fail for want of request.

Help is at hand, help is available yet perhaps due to pride, fear or even lack of concern it is not requested. So the Doctors do not see these nor hear their complaints.

Society bears the brunt of these untreated ailments as alternate remedial means are sought. For an ailment, unless most trivial, will manifest itself somehow painfully irrespective of the resolute disdain it is accorded by the patient.

To return to the initial point of this brief discourse.

A penchant for certain activities would have a root, or root cause somewhere. Or so it would seem.

Does alcohol seek the sot?

The bordello the licentious?

Is the answer important?

Possibly not once again one may consider. What is of greater import is the nature of the activity, and as the Doctor would say affect upon the patient.

People act in different ways in different circumstance. Inner demons freed through the mindlessness of excess, or indulgence of anonymity.

Those who seek the company of strangers, or arms thereof granted a freedom not available within the confines of those they would consider close.

Dark deeds.

Dark places.

Existing in the world of anonymia. A land as sprawling and endless, growing by day as the atlas of the world was so slowly filled over so many years.

For those who exist somewhere, Anonymia is an unknown. It beckons and sits around the next corner away from the prying eyes of those with whom they regularly consort.

It is unlike Nowhere, for Anonymia is sometimes sought but always readily available. Such is the breadth and diversity of this Earth.

Anonymia exists and is a place of abundance.

A place of excess.

A place of freedom.

Lest you are found, and it should disappear revealing that more natural world.

This Earth.

For some there is not a desire to find Anonymia, but a yearning to be known.

To be revealed.

It is their way, and Anonymia is a place they abhor.

So what then is your tendency?

PIRASEA

Hoist the Jolly Roger

throw the deadly plank

these seas belong to us

we take not request

Hoist the Jolly Roger

set the mizzen sail

a course for adventure

and loot for all

Hoist the Jolly Roger

Davey Jones bedamned

spit in Death's eye

a life's cursed path

Hoist the Jolly Roger

cannons to the left

blast those defenders

and take what is theirs

Hoist the Jolly Roger

cutlasses raised

cross the rope bridges

and to Hades set a course

To Hades set a course

ARTIFICE

Is nothing sacred anymore?

A question asked but not usually of some people.

Another place can be found, hidden away behind the doors of many a person and institution that comprises somewhere. It is the place of Artifice, or Artificio for the sake of written gesture.

Here falsity and falsehood bely the exterior visage which comprises society.

Much has been built in Artificio. Like the galleries of the grand masters it hordes its treasures and boasts of itself in grandiose manner.

One of Artificio's most interesting characteristics is that it is paradox and contradiction combined. Artificio exists and is played in so many quarters that it is reality. And reality Artificio.

Such is the genius of humanity that it could concoct for itself this level of contrariness, and resolve it into normalcy. 'The Norm' for such is the foolishness of humanity that it has by necessity required of itself to exist in such a haphazard and graceless manner.

So how does a person find themselves on the road to Artificio?

Possibly via circumstance, another place that exists only temporarily before collapsing again into itself to be replaced by another of its kin.

Circumstance is both a part of Somewhere and Nowhere, a form of bridge between these worlds managing to exist in both. And as such circumstance is an entity in itself, a member of this Earth and part of its fabric.

Artificio deals with circumstance, weaving it deftly like those grand masters into structures and patterns enabling Somewhere to operate in an 'organised' fashion.

For organisation is key, and organisation deals with circumstance like a poor cousin, treating it with contempt for daring to undermine its authority. In the ladder of the tree of life Organisation was breathed life by its inhabitants.

Circumstance being thrust further into the background where Organisation could stand upon it choking its attempts to thwart its authority.

It is a battle for supremacy.

Enough of this though. Artifice exists in an altogether different form. Over many a year Somewhere has developed through the skill and craftsmanship of humanity.

The artisan, those tradesman who chip and chisel slowly sculpting masonry into form. What is form?

Form is shape, and belonging once again to those halcyon days and prior to such in the ages of empires form and elegance were the trappings of power and place.

Pyramids and temples. Then courts and museums. Fronted with form.

Time on this Earth is in itself a member of Artificio. Wielding its guile through the attempts to defy it. Where is that fountain of youth or the Holy Grail? Time gracefully plying its trade enabling humanity the luxury to develop 'form', while stealing the very essence and life from those who inhabit this Earth.

Those magnificent establishments whose form lures visitors and cameras. Whose visage is crafted such by the artisan as to be likened to a Mona Lisa, with even the crafty smile.

Time renders Artificio a place as behind these visages as fire, use and simple age like the internal workings of humanity attempt to lay them to eternal rest.

Humanity is stubborn though. It will not easily allow time to strip away its own quest for if not longer mortality, immortality. And so as humanity has sought to conquer time, it also seeks to stem the tide of time on those places it has come to cherish.

Artificio is rendered again by humanity and those beauteous visages mounted and scaffolded, the internal organs so atrophied as to be beyond repair replaced anew.

The visitors return, stories of place are maintained and Organisation once again takes hold. Orderly queues, orderly minds take in these grand forms, these visages not knowing or caring that they represent a façade for the different machinations within.

So where to now, where to from here?

If Artifice is to be found in such profundity where does one find actuality? And is actuality a place one would desire to visit?

Something for later consideration perhaps, our travels wending their way from Somewhere to already such a wealth of locations that Nowhere is appearing all the more difficult to find.

Like the quest for the Fountain of Youth this quest shall also continue. Resolute and unyielding; going Nowhere.

POLLYTICS

"You're bonkers, stark raving . . . ."

    "I'd like to argue that point"

"Ever been to Poly 'ne 'sia"

    "'No, don' Wantcha rather than 'Ne sia"

"What's a Poly gram?"

    "Sounds a tad overweight"

"How about Poly Gamy."

    "Had enough difficulty with one wife."

It's Polly Tics ya know

Polly tics is all

makes the world go round

tells us what to do

It's Polly Tics ya know

makes us laugh

cause all the Polly' tickin

keeps us entertained

It's Polly Tics ya know

is what telly's for

us to get ta know 'em

then vote 'em off

IGNOMINY

The garden gnome is a most interesting, yet slight creature.

Huddling under umbrellas or choking upon those ghastly pipes they provide a relief from the usual geraniums and chrysanthemums that heighten and flourish in such riotous colour.

Of course it is known that garden gnomes can be acquired at no particular cost to add, that little bit of colour and interest to the environment.

In the world of Somewhere, garden gnomes inhabit an unusual place. They are considered of course inanimate, pottery pieces for display.

How then are the many and varied tales of travel, not to mention the multifarious families and familial groupings of garden gnomes to be explained?

How it may be asked?

The world of Somewhere has relentlessly pushed back boundary after boundary until it finally had the ability to cackle and gleefully discern what was and what was not Something.

Fairies.

Goblins.

Gnomes.

Banished to the fanciful realms.

Banished to the realms of disdain.

Exiled from this Earth not physically, but through a discerning knowledge of what was and what was not developed over those many years.

Where then are these realms?

Fanciful and Disdain. Do they belong Somewhere. They are not like Artificio which renders itself falsely, no they are places that are which are not.

Those who have inhabited the realms of Fanciful and Disdain have done so for many a year, and so these realms are well developed. Like those edifices artfully rendered in time Fanciful and Disdain are inhabited by a grouping of humanity unlike many another.

What is of interest regarding Fanciful and Disdain, rather than Artificio or even Somewhere is perspective. An unusual way which differs from Circumstance in that rather than providing a transient and momentary path it is more fixed, yet flexible.

Perspective is a most unusual way in that even as it is traversed it varies and provides most unusual views of the 'where' within Fanciful and Disdain to both those within and those without.

Where perspective developed is a most interesting topic. Circumstance providing the usual events that ravelled and unravelled to capture and banish those who comprise the communities of Fanciful and Disdain. Garden gnomes, considered inanimate unlike the Fairies and Goblins themselves would seem to exist.

This of course is contrary to the view of non-existence as for the Garden Gnome to be 'considered' as inhabiting either Fanciful or Disdain then it requires perspective. And as perspective is what renders those other creatures banished to these realms a place, the Garden gnome sheds it skin and assumes a place of reality amidst those others.

Garden gnomes have spent many a year finding their own niche within the everyday places inhabited by those who would consider them their owners.

This concept is uniquely human. That other species, in their entirety are subject to human domestication or even ownership is a most unnerving and one would think almost arrogant perspective that humanity has developed of itself.

The pet dog, and human owner wielding the leash. Humanity stamping its authority and its jurisdiction. This perspective may seem 'fair' as humanity has charted its own course, only occasionally assisted by these faithful pets over the course of its history.

So the tree of life finds itself a totem pole, rendering the superior and inferior species in an order. That order being discerned over time by the difference strengths, weaknesses and Somewhere's of the respective groupings.

Those who find themselves Nowhere of course find perspective to be a most familiar view. For from Nowhere perspective is all important and even Somewhere renders itself visible. Although in some cases only partially so, a form perhaps of 'Whereish' myopia for want of a better description.

Garden gnomes are of course Somewhere, and may potentially not comprehend the existence of Nowhere inhabiting a realm slightly at odds with Fanciful and Disdain.

Thus as we traipse past Organisation and are buffeted by circumstance perspective thrusts its jaw, daring those who should encounter it on their way Somewhere to challenge or contradict its view.

TIP TOW

A gentle step

now on your toes

sliiide

bow

Oh elegant one

how training goes

exeeert

slow

Now the prom

to show it all

leeearn

show

So slowly turn

to be visible

waaatch

grow

Gentle step

one then more

tip toe beauty

dance the floor

ALTERNATES

Now we enter a place that is simply, well wrong.

And it is time for that question, most irritable, why?

Not why is the place wrong, but why does it exist. This is an Alternate locale, a Somewhere that exists in so many forms as to make one wonder, should two wrongs not make a right, could it be possible that such a multitude of wrongs may in fact have somehow remarkably managed to achieve just that.

Logic rubs shoulders with perspective and argues blindly that contrariness and contradiction are not problematic, simply stubborn.

So wrong can be righted?

Only, one may wonder if wrong was wrong to begin with. If in fact wrong was right to begin with then should you end up Somewhere wrong, well that would be alright?

How could wrong be right though, this is the stuff of nonsense. Nonsense lacking altogether foresight, hindsight and any other notion that would seem to engender concepts relating to well, wrongness or sensibility.

Alterianation, the process of discovering Somewhere or Something alternate, or alternative. These of course logically should not exist as it has been ascertained over time that Somewhere or Something right will triumph over wrong, hence rendering wrong irrelevant or perhaps illegitimate.

It would then seem irrational that Alterianation as a process could exist when what it derives is wrong, and should not be Somewhere as it is not right.

How then did Somewhere lose its way? As surely this must have been the case for Somewhere alternate to exist and not be wrong, simply Somewhere else.

That being the nett result of these ruminations, Somewhere wrong not being Somewhere wrong simply due to it being designated as alternate, or alternative to what is right.

So Somewhere wrong ends up simply being Somewhere else. How then amidst all these myriad Somewhere's that now comprise this Earth is one to ascertain which is Somewhere right and which is Somewhere wrong?

This may seem to be going Nowhere, which was where this book began and with all these various arguments it is becoming increasingly obvious how in fact a person could in fact find themselves Nowhere. Which now could rationally be described simply as Somewhere else.

If, like Fanciful and Disdain these alternates exist, and co-exist with Somewhere right, is not the likelihood of persons stumbling upon such locales or concepts itself rendering by virtue of chance alone, should chance ever be accorded virtue, potentially rendering the possibility of creating the illusion of reality amidst these alternates.

Somewhere else, being simply that, Somewhere else and having prima facie the same level of perceptual veracity as that Somewhere which is 'known' to be right.

Now we have reached the crux of the matter. How is it then that if Somewhere right is "known" to be right, and Somewhere else "known" to be wrong, that Somewhere else came into and remained in existence?

Did circumstance dally with the virtues of chance creating an Alternate 'knowingness' of right?

Chance you are indeed a mischievous being, not surprising then that you traipse your wares amidst the gambling halls of this Earth.

There you have it, to state the obvious, 'known'. Amidst all that discovering and exploring Something rather than Somewhere, as knowledge is a thing not a location, became 'known'. And was 'known' somehow by those who somehow find themselves Somewhere right (these shall be depicted as the Somehow Somewhere Right persona's).

Oddly enough what was 'known' to those who somehow found Somewhere right was not 'known' to those who somehow found themselves somewhere wrong (these shall be depicted as the Somehow Somewhere Wrong persona's).

If something is not 'known' to those who inhabit, for want of a better term, the Somewhere that is Somewhere wrong, then do they in fact inhabit Somewhere right.

And should chance have played a card with fate creating by circumstance a perspective that something known was contradictory, or perhaps even contrary to what was 'known' to those who found themselves Somewhere wrong, how does circumstance unravel itself to right a wrong so to speak.

The mind boggles, and boggles again.

Such complexity concerning what should be so simple, not surprising that the Road to Nowhere may perchance, that most virtuous route, be found. When, a person finds that Somewhere Else can so readily identify itself amidst the Somewhere that is Somewhere right.

SYMPATICO

Sympatico lend your ears
sympatico a shoulder to cry
sympatico do you weep
for what you have become

Sympatico is your call
sympatico look at us then
sympatico smile on us
such dreadful dreadful events

Sympatico need you us
sympatico do you still want
sympatico leering look
is it this time you offend

Sympatico take a hold

sympatico have your way

sympatico jeer and snarl

a most interesting place

Sympatico

Sympati

what is it you do seek

MONETARY

Home may be where the heart is, but have you ever attended a coronial inquest? This by necessity is used as a means to an end. That end being to ascertain the answer to questions like that posed above. What happened and what went wrong types of questions.

Where does one find these, in a place called quandary.

Quandary abounds and resides within the minds and perspectives of many Somewheres and Someones.

To resolve this in part, and whether or not home is simply where the heart is Humanity entered Monyterry. A form of existence, that like the artisan forged form of those grand edifices created itself as a labyrinthine serpentine behemoth.

Monyterry is so large it veritably, what a fabulous cheery term, veritably envelopes all of Somewhere on this Earth.

Space has the luxury, from at least the current limited and confirmed perspective of humanity of remaining that, space and as such it can only be assumed that Monyterry has not indeed stretched its own boundaries into even that domain such is its enormity.

So where does this apply to such simple concepts as those of Someone Somewhere? The coronial inquest may find, and indeed has on many an occasion that the Monyterry existence resolved and interplayed itself into the reality and circumstance inhabited by someone Somewhere in a detrimental fashion.

Monyterry has this as one of its many characteristics. The landscapes forged by it within Somewhere creating rifts of character and mountains of chagrin.

So from whence did Monyterry spring? How did Somewhere find itself in the grips of Monyterry when Somewhere is itself so vast?

Monyterry exists not in physical form, although there are physical manifestations of it, but permeates the fabric of

Somewhere. It is interesting to note that Monyterry and Nowhere, usually although once again and like always there are exceptions, do not mingle and cohort in a manner as Organised as with Somewhere.

Monyterry and Nowhere tend to function along the lines of circumstance, with chance the virtuous playing a strong hand in the game of cards that is life.

Chance has a playmate in Monyterry, a Somewhere as esoteric as Monyterry itself and so chance and Monyterry mingle gleefully and through folly can resolve themselves into Nowhere.

Can Nowhere exist in the absence of Monyterry, does Monyterry somehow form such a basic building block of Somewhere that even Nowhere would crumble in its absence?

Possibly, for Nowhere is a most unusual place. And most unusual places tend to have properties perhaps, in days before even those bygone halcyon days, mystical. For to survive in Nowhere is something of an art.

To the here and now.

Monyterry exudes the Confidence and Bravado so lacking from Disdain and Fanciful. While having an intrinsic characteristic that is playful Monyterry also has a serious side.

Perspective once again providing a countenance that enables Monyterry visibility different in differing Somewheres. For Monyterry is like the seas, vast and tumultuous. Wild, yet like the tides organised.

More contradictions.

How is it then that someone can be said to inhabit the realms of Monyterry, they are not physical and not Somewhere? Here the fantastical is to be found, duality. Twice existence at the same time. Someone's inhabiting and existing in the realm of Monyterry concurrently with their existence Somewhere. Here being one of Monyterry's cleverer ruses, yes ruses.

Why a ruse? as it is apparent, unlike circumstance or perspective apparently differs in that it is not actual, while being actual.

This is how someone apparently exists Somewhere while not inhabiting, but indulging, in the seas of Monyterry. Riding the surges and plunging through the swales. Another rollercoaster that somehow, apparently, is ridden concurrently with the rollercoaster that is life.

Returning us to those not apparent, but actual realms, the realms of Somewhere. Actual and physical where, even irrespective of the apparent and persistent presence of Monyterry roller coasters are ridden like some great beast most regularly.

These roller coasters plunging through life, like those plunges through the seas of Monyterry leading Somewhere, and perhaps in unfortunate cases, Nowhere.

THERE

You will you MUST

the despot said

You will you MUST

the despot said

Round round the Maypole

round round it goes

you will you MUST

the despot said

Here in lallulia

here lallulia be

join celebration

lallulia lulia le

Makin' our Utopia

beauteous place

made of the ONE

forged as said

You will you MUST

the despot said

There you are

Is there where you want to be?

ADVENTURE

Adventia exists high atop a plateau.

Unlike Monyterry Adventia does not dip nor ebb but retains its lofty place.

A Somewhere most interesting, and a Somewhere traversed in a most haphazard fashion.

Adventia disregards Organisation favouring Circumstance and rending Perspective a passenger as it careens along.

How does someone locate Adventia, as it is a lofty place then it would seem readily identifiable. Yet like those gargantuan mountains would require scaling in the first instance one may assume.

An ill prepared, or unfit someone desiring to scale the peaks of Adventia may fail at the first climb. Perishing in the arms of Calamity, the mistress of Adventia.

What of it then?

Adventia mixes with Adren A Lyn to provide a cocktail that stimulates the senses, making Dizzy and Delirious cohorts. One cavorts with Adventia, intoxicated by these rushes charging again and again along those lofty peaks, not fearing nor wanting to descend.

Like the dependent drug user Adventia lures, intoxicates and then holds captive those who should find their way there.

What of this then, this Somewhere. Most assuredly a long long way from Nowhere. Is it relevant then, pertinent to our discussion?

Indeed it is as the discussion relates to the positioning, relative that it may be of Nowhere to Anywhere.

Anywhere of course has not to this point been encountered as it is somewhat broad. Expansive.

Somewhere was of course the more logical starting point in considering the potential direction to, and understanding of locating Nowhere.

Now we find ourselves in Adventia. Can Adventia be found Anywhere, no it is a Somewhere and requires locating rather than simply being available upon request.

That is, or was of course, in the halcyon days. Now Adventia exists but in a Virtual sense. So those intoxicating realms and heady sensations are available to even the most unassuming, cloaked in virtual guises electronic Adventia can be had, and rehad.

A brave new world, full of the narcosis and conceptual guise of Adventia from within the confines of smaller edifices than those grand locations so carefully sculpted by those artisans so long ago.

Electronic Adventia is more than Somewhere, more than Anywhere? Are Esoteria we find here, the esoteric pondering of whether Anywhere could be considered to be within the vast landscape of Electronic Adventia.

And as Anywhere could theoretically, or notionally due to the constructed virtual nature of itself be found within Electronic Adventia, then it is not surprising to hear from some people the unusual statement that they have not been Anywhere.

For surely each and every one of us must have been Somewhere, so what is it that would make one think they had not been Anywhere?

Adventia.

That longing and desirous state, yearning. For Adventia has another altogether more sinister side, Comparison. This differing from Perspective as Comparison is quantifiable, measurable and competitive.

So Adventia plays upon that yearning to be noticed, the thrill of the chase, and telling of the tale. So those who have not been Anywhere have been Somewhere yet not of sufficient heights as to be considered part of Adventias landscape.

Adventias landscapes are like battlements, protecting themselves from accidental intrusion. Electronic Adventia circumvents this, providing the unusual luxury of mitigated risk while enabling conceptually those who desire so to be transported Anywhere.

So Esoteria have we now convinced ourselves that Electronic artificial Anywhere is in its vastness now so grand as to encapsulate Adventia and Somewhere combined.

Is Nowhere then to be found in the vastness of this landscape. The forbidding territory sculpted by Humanities creative talents to potentially and theoretically be so grand as to have a scale comparable to Anywhere.

Humanities achievement, Adventia available to all who seek those intoxicating times and on a scale comparable to Anywhere itself.

Staggering, humanity has certainly outdone itself.

Anyone for Adventia?

XTRA

A little bit more

that extra bit

why not extra terrestrial

oh do not be so

extra vagant

That touch

that extra bit

seemingly extra neous

or something

extra ordinary

Please then

that extra bit

outwardly extra verted

then maybe

extra curriculur

The things we do

Games we play

Extra Extra

Read all about it

No, not today

FINISH

Everything must have an end.

So after discovering Anywhere, and that having not been Anywhere can be circumvented by virtually going Anywhere MUST everything have an end?

Like the dog chases its tail, the search for Nowhere has lead from Somewhere to Anywhere. Only to find that Anywhere itself has now been created by Humanity.

Is it possible then that Humanity can exist Anywhere, and within the virtual Anywhere it has created exist without end?

To be stored as an entity within an entity, accessible for Adventia or just perhaps a visit by someone professing not to have been Anywhere and desiring to go there.

The Fountain Of Youth, poured in silicone and rendered in binary.

Is this Hubris? Hubris unlike Disdain and Fanciful an extravagance and jeering in the face of the inevitable. The escape of Death, whose scythe cuts swathes through Mortality with such abandon.

Humanity defeats its arch nemesis.

Or does this fly in the face of conviction, the concept of belief or faith bestowed upon those who as described previously 'know' what they 'know', those Somehow Somewhere Right persona's.

Does the significance of this 'knowing' so long established place the concern and even concept of 'defeating' death by rendering an artificial existence not Hubris, but irrelevant?

Is, in the End the legendary land of Atlantis more than a myth, fable as told by Plato? Do realms of advanced yet lost civilisations ring true requiring nought but location?

What path to such a destination, via Hubris or some other more arcane method?

Is it then that people are seeking the answer to a question that is already known to them. In which case why do they seek it? Or is it that while the answer is known, the path is not so readily followed nor understood. Perhaps, like Atlantis the path has been covered and transformed into a landscape that, like Adventia even sits atop and amidst a landscape too difficult for some to traverse.

Atlantis where are you?

Hidden beneath layers and layers of impenetrable jungle and across vast seas.

Atlantis where are you?

Lost, unlike perhaps the sought for answer to Eternity, but in a virtual landscape as contrived and complex as the electronic Anywhere devised in so recent a time.

This Somewhere, requiring to be traversed to a destination understood but a path potentially unknown. A hidden path as mystical and enchanted as the destination to which it portends to lead.

Fanciful and Disdain are not part of this mystical way, they have an enchantment, but an enchantment of their own. So magic it may be said, unlike the virtuality that is electronic Anywhere exists in reality.

Mysticism and shamanism of old transformed and transfigured beyond those stage illusions to physical form. Miraculous.

Perhaps.

Where does this leave us?

Nowhere.

Another Nowhere.

A Nowhere without a start, but with a destination. For it is interesting that while Anywhere encompasses all, including even Atlantis, Nowhere also requires an understanding of direction.

In the end, where was I?

Nowhere as at the beginning.

To traverse the lands of Nowhere differs from Adventia or even Somewhere. Nowhere lacks feature, distinguishing landmark. Direction is difficult.

And so in a manner akin to locating Atlantis, the path from Nowhere must first have direction. Bearings.

How are these to be found, is there a trail like bread crumbs scattered or thread unfurled?

Adventia is reckless, Somewhere is comprehended but Nowhere requires tact, skill and caution.

It is not for the reckless, nor the faint-hearted for demons lurk here.

So, where was I?

Finding my bearings, on a slow cautious path not bound for Atlantis, but Somewhere. Which is better than Nowhere.

So there is an end after all, FINIS.

A place to put the thoughts of Nowhere to rest, and for Somewhere to reside. It could be Anywhere.

To the others on life's journey, see you on the trails.

THE END